JAMES

PERCY

MEET ALL THESE FRIENDS IN BUZZ BOOKS:

Thomas the Tank Engine
The Animals of Farthing Wood
Biker Mice from Mars
Winnie-the-Pooh
Fireman Sam
Rupert
Babar

First published in Great Britain 1994 by Buzz Books
an imprint of Reed Children's Books
Michelin House, 81 Fulham Road, London SW3 6RB
and Auckland, Melbourne, Singapore and Toronto
Reprinted 1995

ISBN 1 85591 330 5

Printed and bound in Italy by Olivotto

HENRY'S FOREST

buzz books

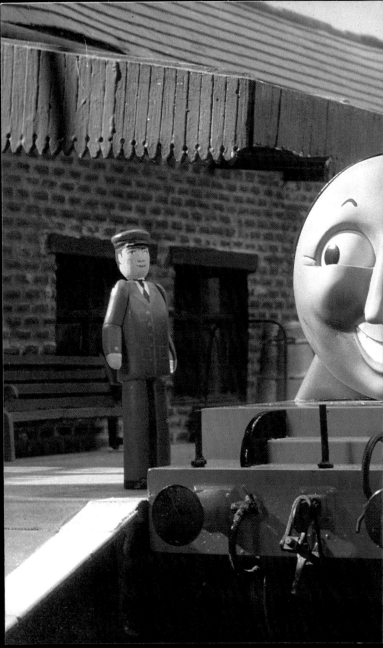

Henry the Green Engine has lived on the Island of Sodor for many years. He wouldn't want to be anywhere else.

He likes every part of it, from the fields filled with flowers to the white, sandy beaches, but there is one place that Henry always enjoyed visiting more than any other.

His driver knew this too.

"Come on, Henry," he would say.
"We've made good time today. We'll
stop for a while by the forest."

Henry loved it here. The forest was full of broad oaks and tall pines.

Henry could remember the day, long ago, when he and Toby brought some new trees to be planted, and Terence and Trevor helped haul them into place.

Now he could see the trees growing amongst the others on the hillside.

Henry always felt better for being here. He couldn't really explain why, but his driver understood.

"It's peaceful," he said to Henry.

But one night everything changed.

The engines were resting in the shed.

"Listen," said Thomas. "Can you hear a strange whistling sound?"

"It's the wind blowing outside our shed," replied Toby, "but I've never heard it like this before."

"Do you know," added James, "if Gordon wasn't here now, I'd say it was him thundering by with the express."

All the engines laughed, except Henry.

"I hope the wind won't harm the forest!"

By morning, the fierce winds had gone
but the damage was done.

Henry's driver came to see him in the yard.

"Trees have fallen on the line. We must
help clear the tracks."

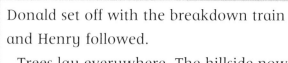

Donald set off with the breakdown train
and Henry followed.

Trees lay everywhere. The hillside now
looked so bare.

Henry felt sad.

"What will happen to all the animals who live here?" he thought.

When Henry's flat trucks were full of logs, he took them to the timber mill where they would

be turned into furniture and other things.

Henry was glad the wood was being put to good use, but he was still sorry to lose part of his forest.

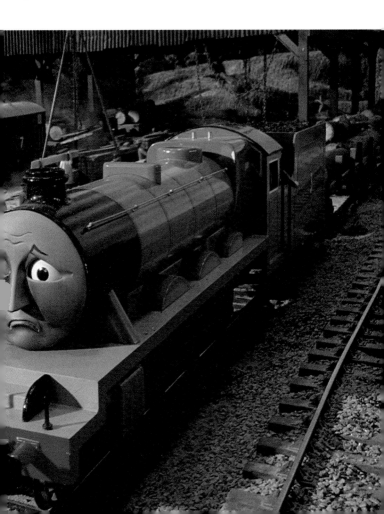

"Oh dear!" sighed Toby. "I wish there was something we could do to make things better again."

"Yes indeed!" replied Thomas. "But what? We can't mend broken trees!"

Toby puffed slowly into the yard.

"Hello, Toby," said the Fat Controller.
"You do look glum."

"I'm sad about the trees," said Toby.
"And so is Henry. The forest is a special
place to him. Now some of it is gone."

21

"We'll soon put that right. I have an important job for you, Toby. I would like you to take some trucks to the forest."

When the trucks arrived, Toby was delighted.

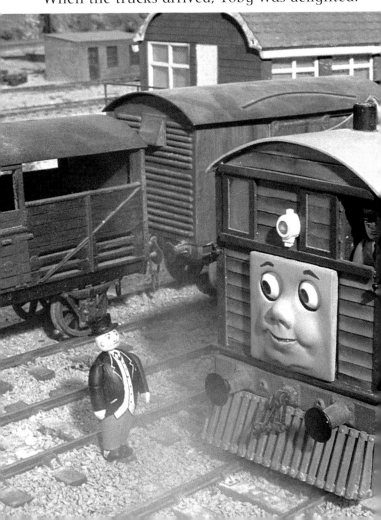

They were full of splendid, young trees, all ready for planting.

"This is the best job I've ever had," said Toby happily.

When Henry returned, he was most surprised.
There were Trevor and Terence busily
helping the workmen clear the torn stumps
and branches.

24

"Look, Henry!" called Terence. "We're
beginning again. The hillside will look better
than ever before. You'll see!"

Now Henry can see the trees growing strong and tall, and the animals are coming back.

Sometimes everywhere is quiet. At other times, Henry can hear leaves rustling or a bird's wing brushing the air.

Often he can hear the sound of children laughing, and always he is happy here.

THOMAS

EDWARD

GORDON